19.95   **DATE DUE**

DEC 1 9 2007	
JUN 2 5 2008	
OCT 1 6 2009 SEP 0 8 2010	
JUL 2 6 2011	
FEB 2 8 2013	
MAR 2 1 2013 JUL 1 0 2013	
MAR 2 4 2014	
MAY 0 9 2014	
JUN 2 5 2014	
AUG 2 7 2014	

1st grade

Young Peggy

Young Animal Pride Series
Book 13

Cataloging-in-Publication Data

Sargent, Dave, 1941–
    Young peggy / by Dave and Pat Sargent ;
illustrated by Elaine Woodword.—Prairie Grove, AR :
Ozark Publishing, c2005.
    p. cm. (Young animal pride series ; 13)

    "Don't wander off"—Cover.
    SUMMARY : Peggy goes exploring
and finds a friend. They get lost, have
adventures then a friend helps them
find their mamas.
    ISBN 1-56763-887-2 (hc)
          1-56763-888-0 (pbk)

    1. Porcupines—Juvenile fiction.
[1. Porcupines—Fiction.] I. Sargent, Pat, 1936–
II. Woodword, Elaine, 1956– ill.
III. Title. IV. Series.

    PZ10.3.S243Pe 200
    [Fic]—dc21   2004092999

Printed in the United States of America

Young Peggy

Young Animal Pride Series
Book 13

by Dave and Pat Sargent

Illustrated by Elaine Woodword

Ozark Publishing, Inc.
P.O. Box 228
Prairie Grove, AR 72753

Dave and Pat Sargent, authors of the extremely popular Animal Pride Series, visit schools all over the United States, free of charge. If you would like to have Dave and Pat visit your school, please ask your librarian to call 1-800-321-5671.

Foreword

While Peggy is out playing, she goes too far from home and gets lost. She meets Bob. He is a porcupine, too. They have a scary adventure, but finally they find their mothers.

My name is Peggy.

I am a porcupine.

I live in a hollow tree.

I have sharp quills.

I climb trees.

I eat pine tree bark.

Mama went to sleep.

I went out to play.

I climbed a tall tree.

I saw a porcupine like me.

It was Bob.

We ran and played.

We got lost.

We ate some bark. Yuck!

We played on a log.

We rode the rapids.

We bumped into Billy's lodge.

The beaver found our mamas.

They took us home.